LADDIE AND NASH
LEARN TO BAKE

ANITA HINSON CAUTHEN
ILLUSTRATED BY TIM STRINGER

CU00864457

Copyright © 2024 by Anita Hinson Cauthen. All rights reserved.
This book may not be reproduced or stored in whole or in part
by any means without the written permission of the author
except for brief quotations for the purpose of review.

ISBN: 978-1-963569-48-3 (hard cover)
978-1-963569-49-0 (soft cover)

Edited by: Amy Ashby

Published by Warren Publishing
Charlotte, NC
www.warrenpublishing.net
Printed in the United States

To my precious pups—Nash, on Earth and Laddie, in heaven.

Laddie, Nash, and Papa Buck lived a comfortable life. Papa Buck awoke early each morning to drive to his bakery, Buck's Best Batch, where he baked delicious sweets.

Left alone during the day, Laddie and Nash amused themselves with games of hide-and-seek and tug-of-war.

In the evenings, Papa Buck liked to cuddle Laddie and Nash and tell them about the many customers who bought his sweets each day. Still, Laddie and Nash often wondered about Papa Buck's workday at Buck's Best Batch.

One early morning, Papa Buck entered the stillness of the moonlit bedroom. He tiptoed to the beds and gazed lovingly at Laddie and Nash as he whispered softly, "Sweet dreams, my precious babies."

And just like he did every morning before daylight, he kissed them goodbye and hugged them tight.

Then Papa Buck drove his bakery van to Buck's Best Batch to make the daily sweets from scratch.

Later, after breakfast, Laddie and Nash sat at the kitchen table.

Holding a pencil and paper, Laddie exclaimed, "Buck's Best Batch is a place of mystery. Let's plan a trip to learn and see!"

"Oh, Laddie, what fun it will be to explore and sample treats folks adore!" Nash replied as he clapped his front paws.

The next morning, in the wee hours, Papa Buck entered the bedroom to give kisses and hugs. Laddie pretended to sleep, with one eye half open. Nash was asleep on his back, snoring loudly, zzzZZZZ-ZZZZzzz-snrkx-zZZZzzzZZ.

When Laddie heard the front door close, he jumped out of bed and yelled, "Nash, wake up, you sleepy pup! We must race to Papa Buck's place."

After they scampered through the living room, Laddie jumped onto Nash's back to unlock and open the front door.

They heard the bakery van's engine sputter to life as they raced down the driveway. Quickly they grabbed hold of the handles on the van's back door and held on tightly for the windy ride to Buck's Best Batch.

Upon arrival, Papa Buck unlocked the door and walked into the bakery kitchen. His eyes sparkled with anticipation of sweet aromas filling the air.

Laddie and Nash dashed into the room and hid under a table to watch Papa Buck.

Papa Buck stood behind his worktable to begin preparing the day's scrumptious treats. Over the mixer's *whoosh*, *whirr*, and *clickety-clack*, his singsong voice could be heard:

"Scoop, weigh, mix, and bake
cookies, pies, buns, and cakes.
Fresh-baked each day to satisfy
cravings for sweets that gratify!"

After sliding the last pan of cookies onto
the cooling rack, Papa Buck said to himself,
"Cookies, pies, and cakes are baked.
Now a quick lunch and a nap I'll take."

About fifteen minutes later, when they were certain Papa Buck was asleep, Laddie and Nash crawled out from under the table. Looking around in awe, the pups were eager to explore!

Laddie ran to a wall of refrigerators across the room. He opened a door and felt a *swoosh* of cold air. The pans were full of baked cookies and cupcakes.

The naughty pup grabbed a cupcake and took a bite. "OWWW! This cake is frozen! I hope a tooth isn't broken!" he cried.

Meanwhile, Nash poured flour into the mixing bowl as he turned the switch on high. "OHHH! WHOA!" he yelled as a cloud of flour covered him from head to toe.

Laddie ran across the room and turned off the
mixer. Then he said to Nash:
"To the cooling racks!
Hurry up, let's not wait!
You gather cookies,
and I'll gather cakes.

"Let's stand on buckets
to reach up high
    and grab tasty sweets.
Now don't be shy!"
    "Laddie, the racks are
so tall. We could lose our
balance and fall!" Nash
warned as he followed
Laddie to the cooling racks.

SUGA LOUR

Laddie and Nash climbed onto buckets filled with flour and sugar to reach the enticing sweets. As they grasped pans of goodies, the buckets overturned. A loud *bam*, *thud*, *clang*, and *clatter* echoed in the room.

Laddie and Nash sat in the messy pile and munched, crunched, gobbled, and smacked as they devoured the broken treats.

An hour later, Papa Buck walked in
the door and saw the pups lying on
their backs in a big ol' mess, whining
and holding their bloated tummies:
    "Oh me, oh my, look at you two!
    No respect for what I do.
    Eat one sweet for goodness' sake,
    else you'll get a tummy ache!"

Early the next morning, Papa Buck nudged Laddie and Nash awake and said, "Off you go to Buck's Best Batch to learn the trade and bake from scratch."

Nash crawled out of bed and stretched and yawned.

Laddie gazed sleepily at Papa Buck and moaned, "I'm still not feeling my best. Can I stay in bed and rest?"

When Papa Buck glared at him, Laddie jumped out of bed as he wiped the sleep from his eyes.

In the bakery kitchen, Nash stood behind the worktable and scooped sugar to be weighed while Laddie operated the mixer amid the loud *whoosh*, *whirr*, and *clickety-clack*.

Nash reached into a bucket and scooped margarine to add to the bowl of sugar. Then he reached over for a carton of milk, slipped, and fell headfirst into the mixing bowl.

"Baking isn't as easy as it looks," Nash groaned. "Papa Buck, I'll never be a cook!"

Papa Buck rushed over and carried him to the sink to wash off the sticky mess.

Laddie was attempting to separate egg whites from the yellow yolks, with no luck. "Papa Buck, I just can't get it right!"

Then he asked, "Can we make yellow cake instead of white?"

As the two pups baked,
Papa Buck encouraged them.
"Laddie and Nash, don't despair.
Mix the batter smooth and light
as air!"

Then Laddie carefully poured batter into round cake pans. Nash placed the filled cake pans on racks in the huge wall oven across the room as Papa Buck directed, "Cakes in the oven and bake with care until vanilla scents the air."

Thirty minutes later, Nash moved the cake pans to the cooling racks as Laddie scooped, weighed, and mixed the icing to smooth between the layers, on sides, and on top.

CONFECTIONER'S SUGAR

SHORTENING

At the end of the workday, Laddie and Nash sat at the kitchen
table, forks in hand, while Papa Buck cut slices of cake and said:
"Now you know the time it takes
to scoop, weigh, mix, and bake.
Always be proud of what you do
in any work you may pursue."

The next morning when Papa Buck entered the moonlit bedroom, Laddie and Nash smiled in their sleep, dreaming of baking cookies, pies, buns, and cakes.

Tea Ball Cookies

Yield: Approximately 5 dozen cookies

INGREDIENTS:

For Cookies

- 4 ¼ cups bread flour
- 1 ¼ cups granulated sugar
- 1 ¼ cups shortening
- 1 cup margarine
- pinch of salt
- 3 oz. pecans, finely chopped
- 1 tsp. vanilla extract

For Icing

- 3 cups confectioners' sugar
- water (variable)
- Food coloring

DIRECTIONS:

Mixing Cookies

1. Preheat the oven to 350° F.
2. Mix all ingredients together lightly, just enough for the dough to hold together.
3. Shape 2 tsp. of the dough into a ball.
4. Place the dough balls 2 inches apart on a parchment-lined baking sheet.
5. Using your thumb, make a deep indentation in middle of each cookie.
6. Place the baking sheet in the oven for 20–25 minutes until the edges and bottoms are lightly golden brown.

Mixing Icing

1. Slowly add lukewarm water to the confectioners' sugar while stirring until the icing is smooth and stiff. (Do not make icing too stiff because it will become hard and brittle when cooled.)
2. Stir in the food coloring in the desired color.
3. Fill the indentations on top of the baked, cooled cookies and allow an hour for the icing to set.
4. If multiple colors of icing are desired, place confectioners' sugar and water in small bowls and add food coloring as desired.

Milton Keynes UK
Ingram Content Group UK Ltd.
UKHW051132210424
441366UK00005B/15

9 781963 569490